Derble gets in Shape

by: Joel Biggs

Illustrated by: Ginalyn Tirando

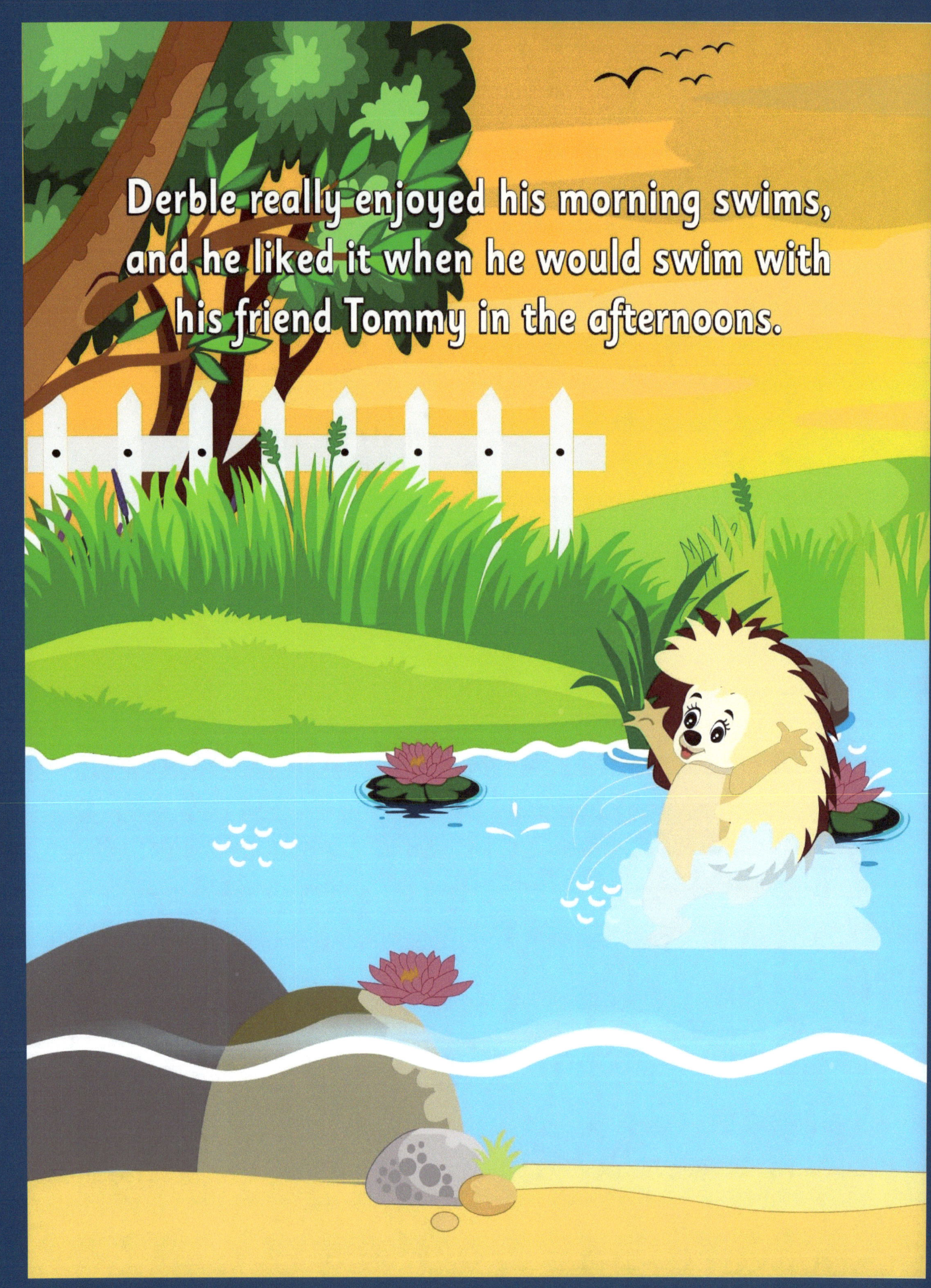
Derble really enjoyed his morning swims,
and he liked it when he would swim with
his friend Tommy in the afternoons.

But today when Derble was walking home
from his morning swim, he noticed
that he was a little more tired
than he normally was.

So Derble thought about it while he was eating his lunch. He wasn't feeling sick, so it had to be something else.

Maybe he wasn't getting enough exercise. He did swim everyday, well, sort of.

Actually he chased bugs,
splashed and played, but
he liked to call it swimming.

Could that be it, could it be that he was just out of shape?

Derble decided that first thing in the morning he would start. First he would run to his favorite swimming place.

Then he would actually swim,
well a few laps anyway.

He still wanted to do his favorite things, but he told himself that he would really swim.

Then he promised himself
that he would run back
home afterwards for lunch.
Derble figured that would
be a good start.

So when Derble woke up, he hopped out of bed, got ready and started to run to his favorite place.

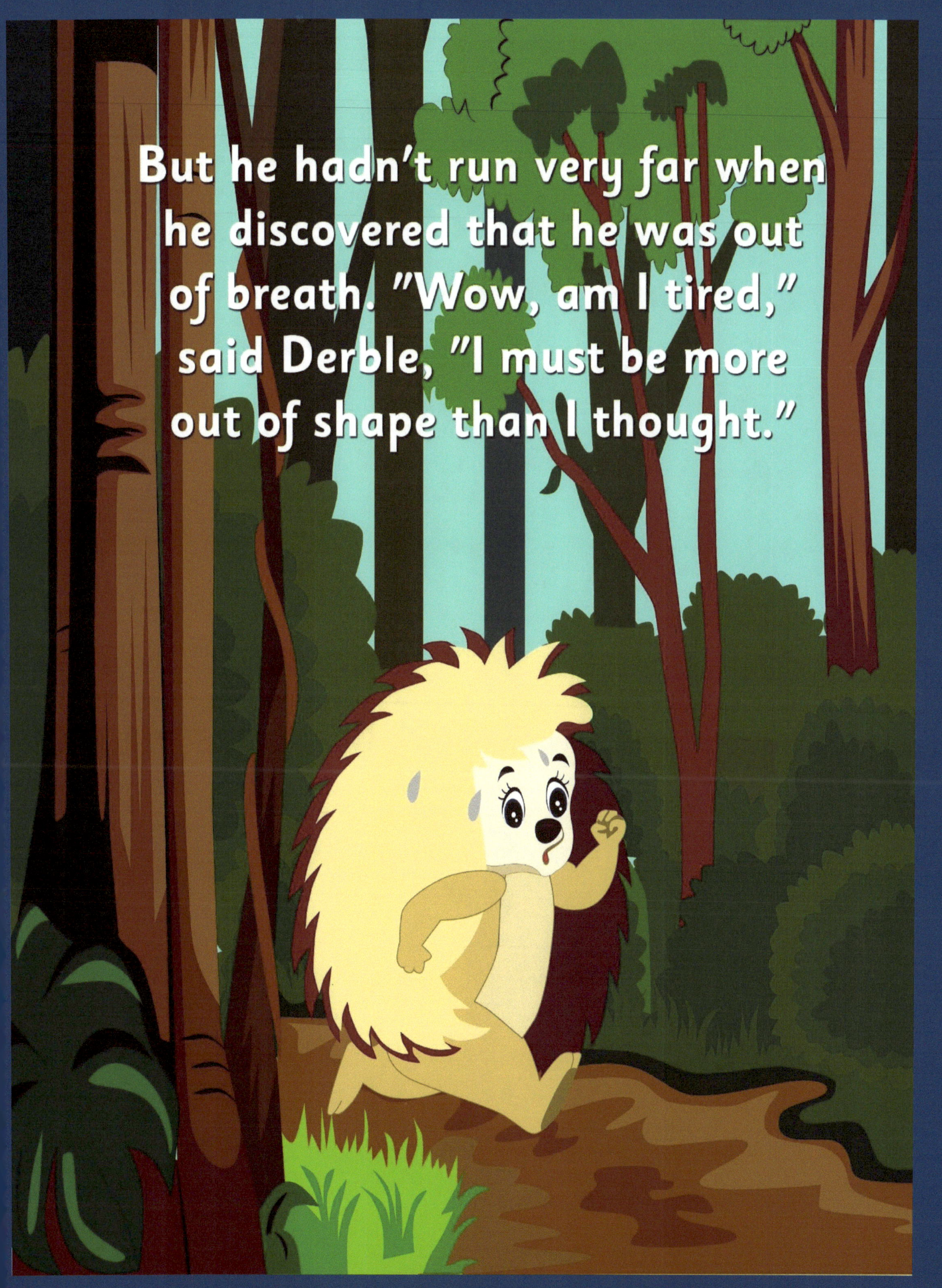

But he hadn't run very far when he discovered that he was out of breath. "Wow, am I tired," said Derble, "I must be more out of shape than I thought."

Derble continued on, but he walked until he caught his breath, then he tried to run again.

But again the same thing happened,
he ran a little bit and then he had
to stop to catch his breath.

So Derble decided that he would just walk the rest of the way.

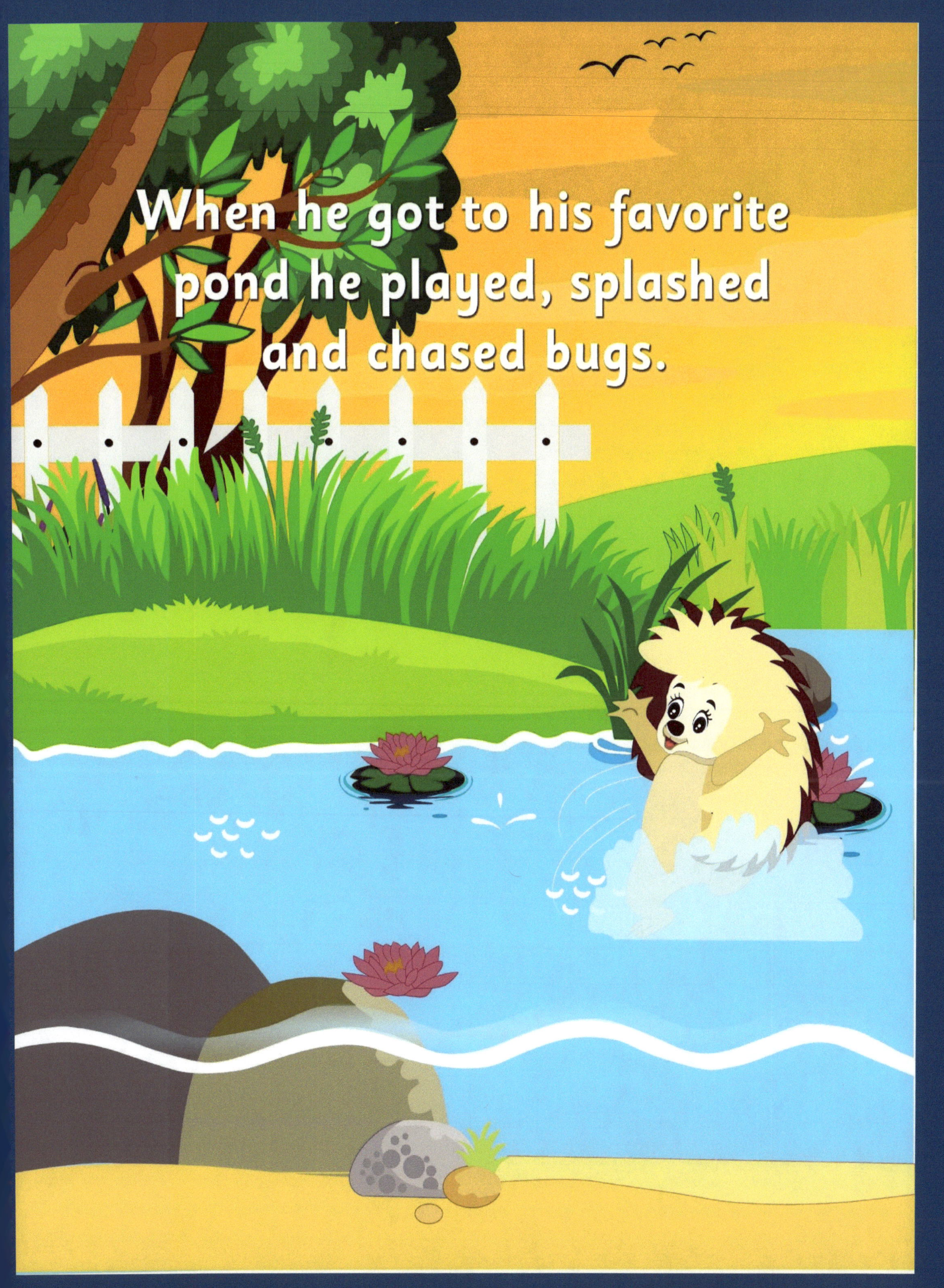

When he got to his favorite pond he played, splashed and chased bugs.

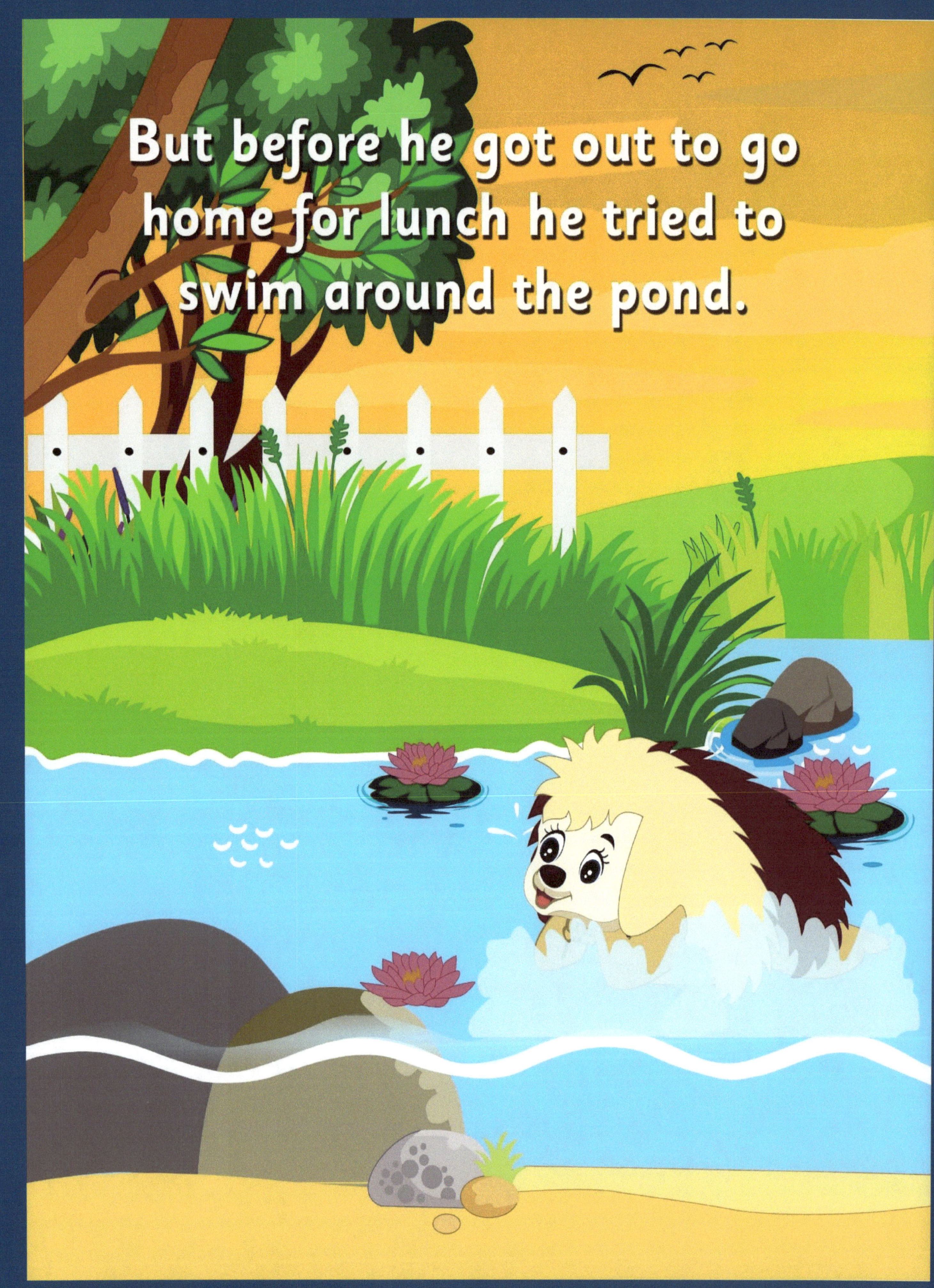
But before he got out to go home for lunch he tried to swim around the pond.

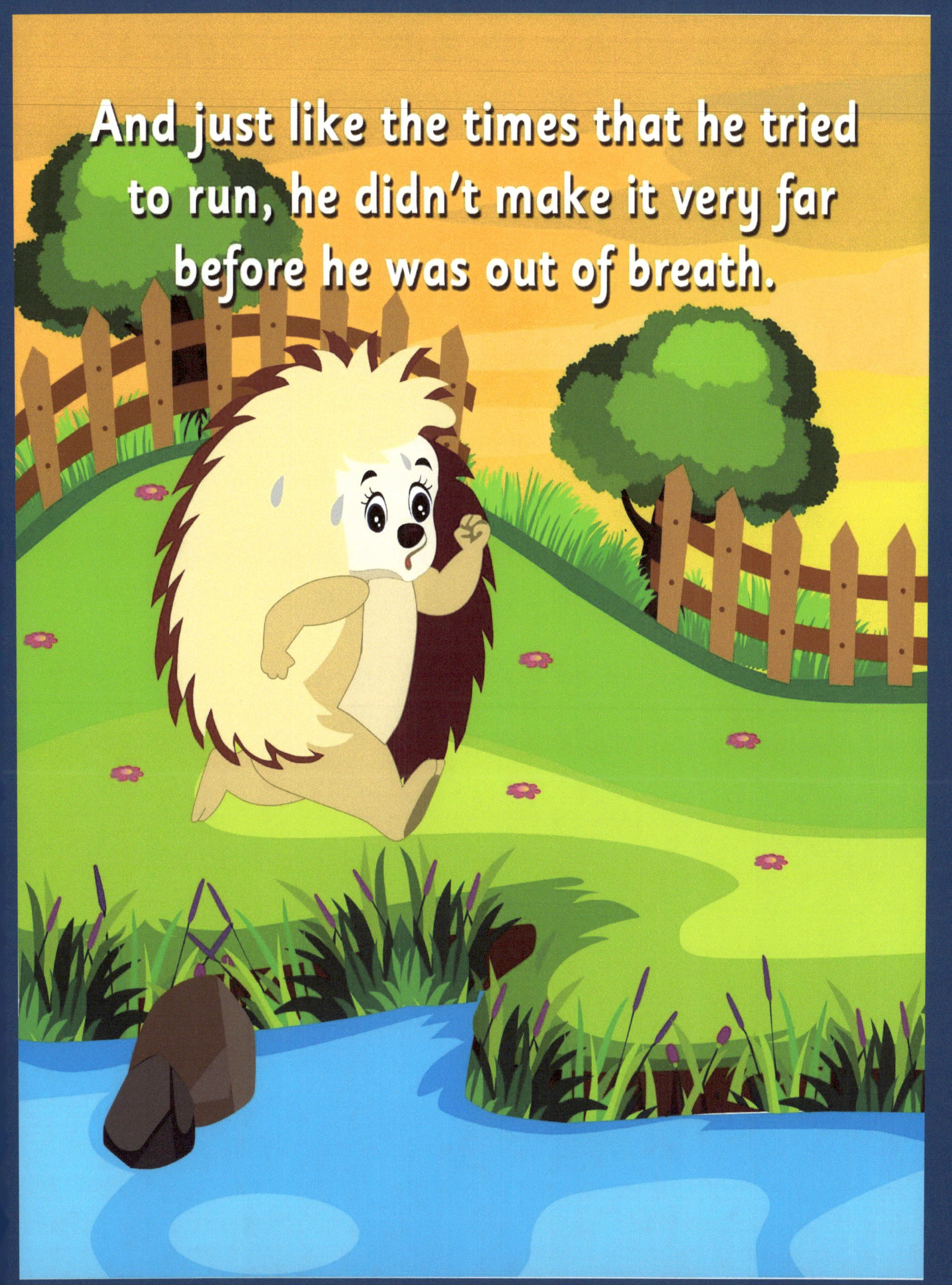
And just like the times that he tried to run, he didn't make it very far before he was out of breath.

When he caught his breath,
he tried again and again
he didn't make it very far.

This made Derble laugh, "I must really be out of shape," Derble said to himself.

On the walk home, he was
even more tired than he
was the day before.

I have to just keep on trying, he thought. I'll just keep trying everyday to go a little bit further than I did the day before.

And before long I'll be back in shape and I won't be as tired as I am now.

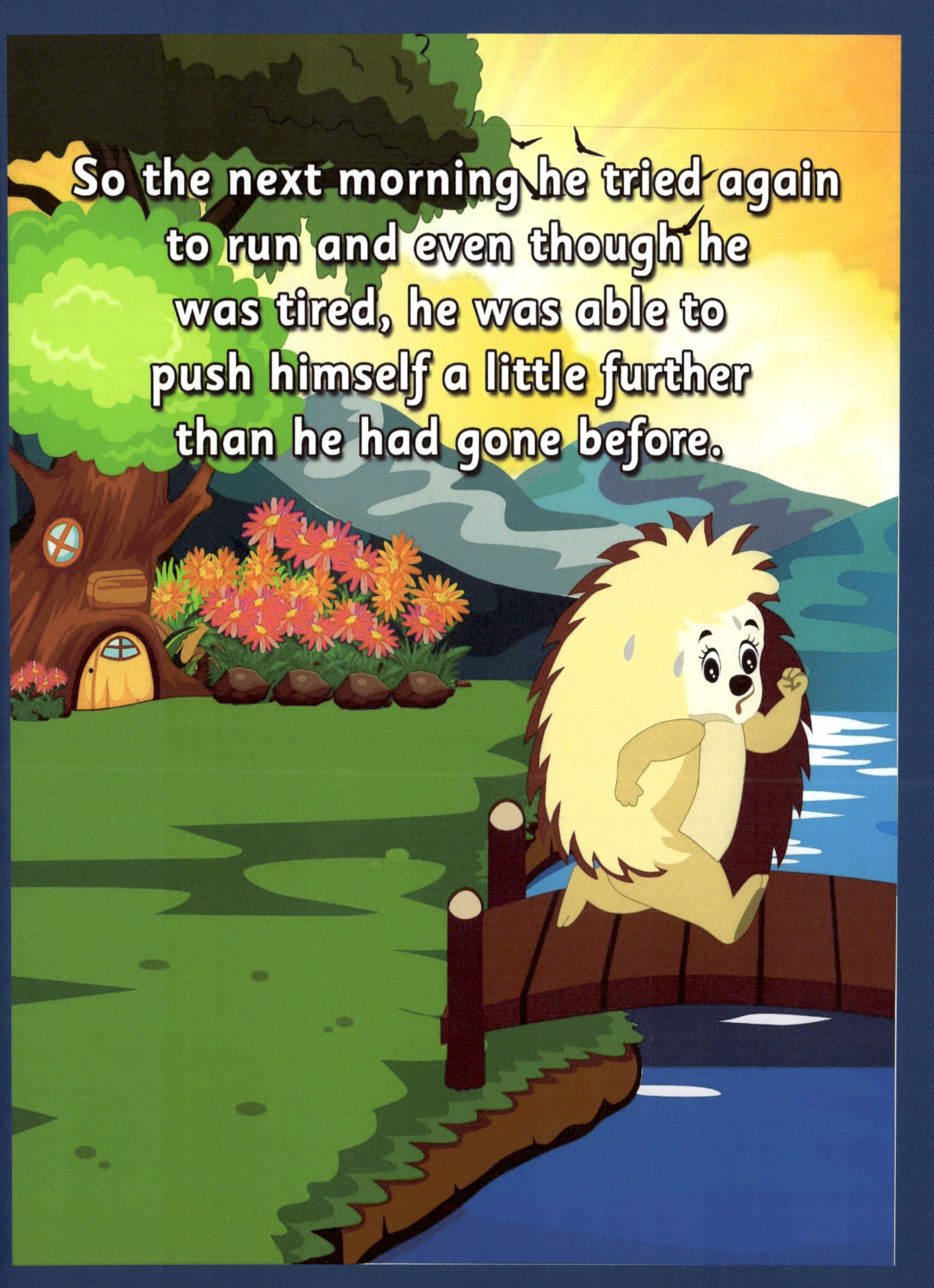
So the next morning he tried again to run and even though he was tired, he was able to push himself a little further than he had gone before.

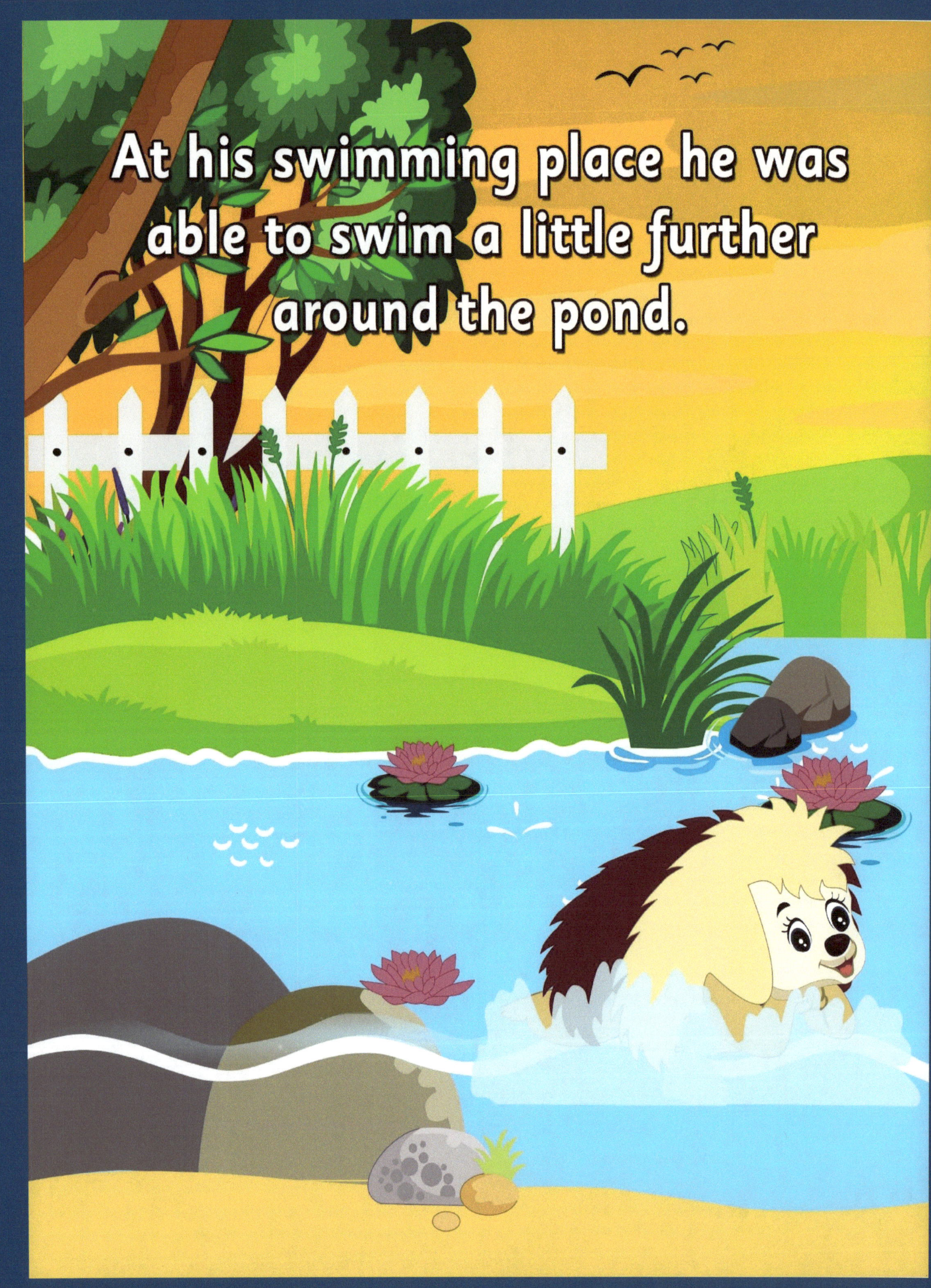
At his swimming place he was able to swim a little further around the pond.

And then he even tried to run
some on the way home.

It wasn't far but it was still further than he had gone the day before.

Derble kept doing a little farther each day
and it did take longer than he had
planned but the day did come.

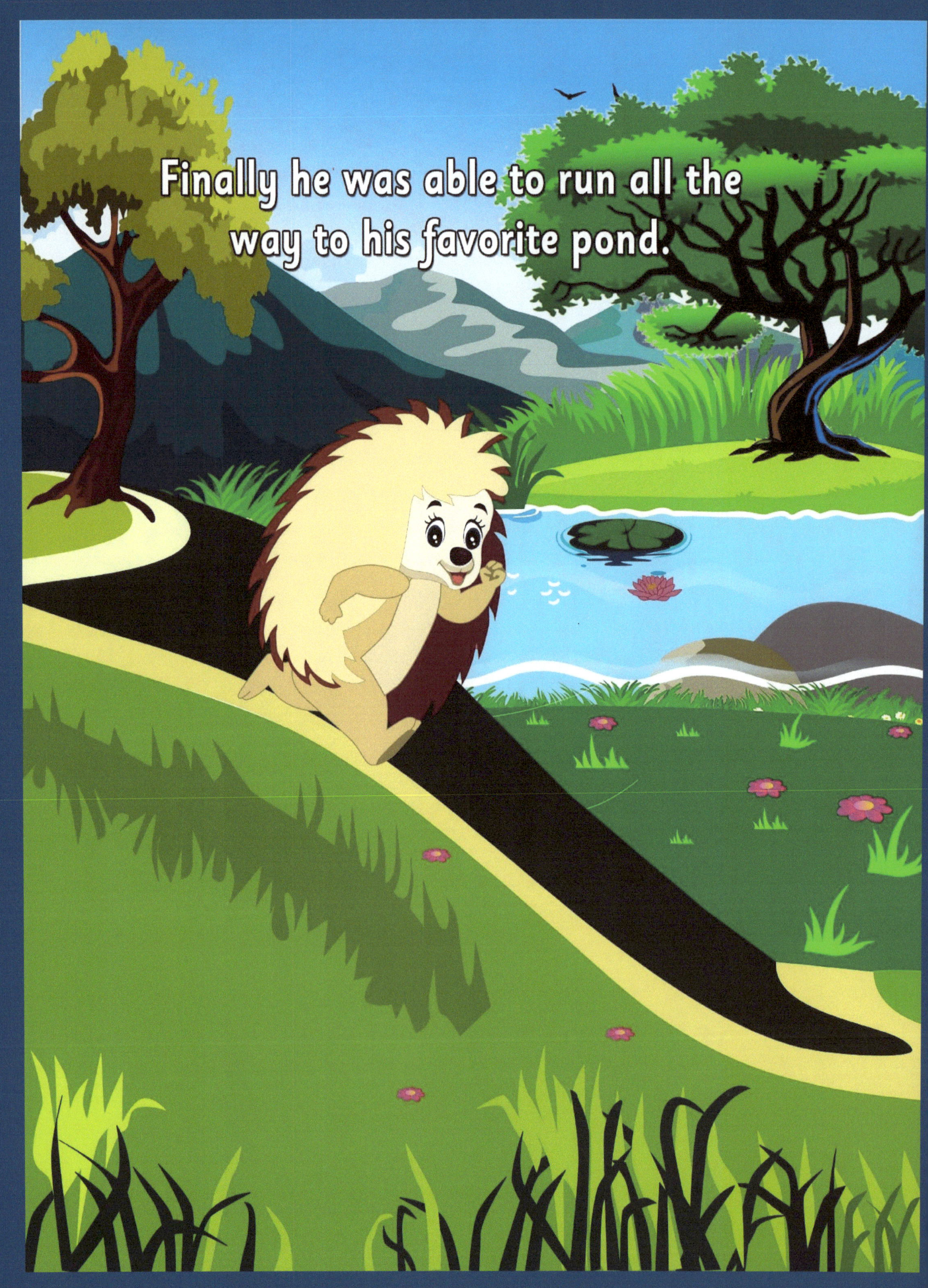

Finally he was able to run all the
way to his favorite pond.

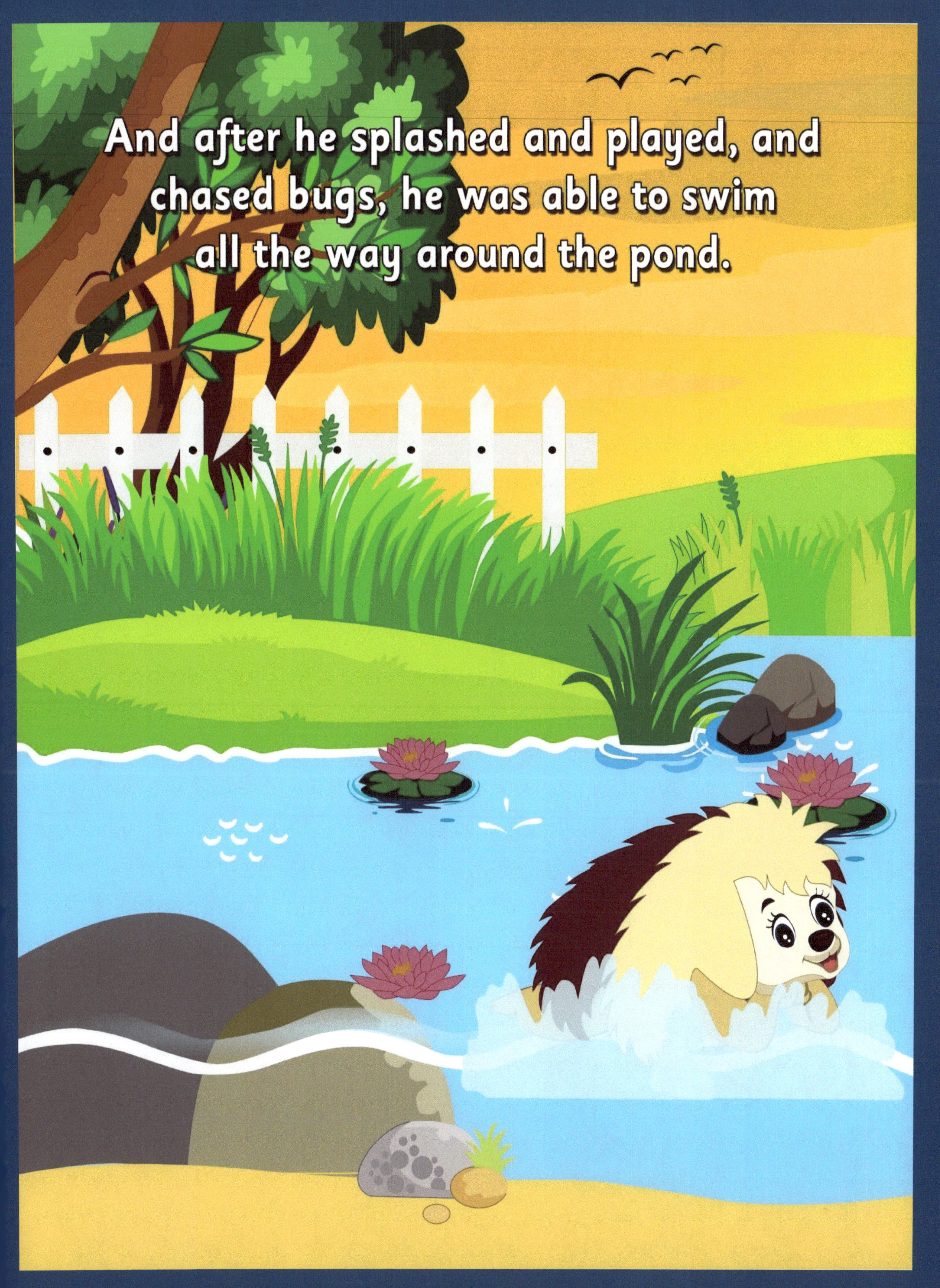

And after he splashed and played, and
chased bugs, he was able to swim
all the way around the pond.

And he was even able to run all the
way back home for lunch.

And it was a good day...